Cannibal Island

The Cave of
the Dead

Exit from Caves

Reefs

Land of the Old Man of the Sea

Monkeys

For Oliver – J.R.
For Tanda, Steve and Matthew – S.F.

First published in Great Britain and the USA in 2007 by
Frances Lincoln Children's Books, 4 Torriano Mews,
Torriano Avenue, London NW5 2RZ
www.franceslincoln.com

British Library Cataloguing in Publication Data available on request

ISBN: 978-1-84507-531-6

Illustrated with pen and ink and acrylics

Set in Meridien

Printed in Singapore

1 3 5 7 9 8 6 4 2

The Seven Voyages of

Sinbad the Sailor

James Riordan

Illustrated by Shelley Fowles

F

FRANCES LINCOLN
CHILDREN'S BOOKS

Fifth Voyage

Sixth Voyage

Seventh Voyage

First Voyage

WHALE ISLAND

Sinbad's father was a wealthy merchant in the great city of Baghdad. He died when his son was still young, and Sinbad soon squandered his father's fortune. Luckily, the young man came to his senses before it was too late and, with what little remained, he bought merchandise and joined a company of merchants.

They sailed from Baghdad down-river to Basra, and from there across the seas. For many weeks they saw nothing but the boundless, ever-changing sea. Then, early one morning, a look-out in the crow's nest shouted, "Land ahoy! An island, with fresh fruit and water!"

The captain dropped anchor in the bay, letting the merchants and crew ashore to stretch their legs. Some filled water-butts, some lit fires to cook a meal or wash their dirty linen in large pots.

Sinbad, meanwhile, wandered through the trees, marvelling at the parrots, humming birds and gaudy blooms. "What a paradise," he sighed, breathing in the perfumed air. "So calm and peaceful."

What was that? Was it his imagination – or did the earth tremble?

There it was again! This time, so strong that men were knocked off their feet.

As Sinbad lay dazed above the shore, he heard the captain yell, "Back to the ship! Save yourselves!"

Men scrambled to safety, abandoning half-eaten meals and half-washed clothes. Many were left stranded as the ship sailed swiftly away. All the while, the island bucked and bounded like an untamed camel.

This was no garden of paradise… It was a giant whale! The monster had evidently slept undisturbed for so long that an entire island had grown upon its back – with date and banana trees, wild flowers and golden sands. The fires had woken it up.

One last time the wounded beast leapt up, tail thrashing the sea…
then it sank like a stone to the ocean bed.

Sinbad found himself struggling in the swell, tossed to and fro
amid rootless trees and drowning men. A seething whirlpool would
have dragged him down, but for a floating washtub. Hauling himself
inside and using his arms as paddles, he rowed for dear life away
from the sunken isle.

RESCUED

Wind and wave finally
drove Sinbad towards cliffs that towered high
above a strange shore. Pulling himself up by creepers,
he reached the cliff-top and fell, exhausted, in a faint.
How long he slept, he could not tell. But when he awoke,
the burning sun was right above him. With feet torn
and bleeding from the climb, he dragged himself
along until he overlooked a plain sloping down to
the distant sea. "If I reach that valley," he told
himself, "I can eat and rest, and watch
out for passing ships."

Somehow he slithered down the slope, and was able to feed on figs
and dates and quench his thirst from freshwater streams. When he'd
rested, he hobbled to the shore and scanned the horizon.

Months passed.

One day – Allah be praised – a ship entered the bay and sailors came ashore. To Sinbad's delight, it was the same ship he'd boarded at Basra. He rushed to meet the captain, who did not recognise the ragged castaway. After hearing Sinbad's story, the captain told his own tale:

"Good fortune favoured our trade. What a pity that so many noble merchants drowned – their wares still lie in my hold."

With fast-beating heart, Sinbad asked, "Who were the merchants?"

"Oh, gentlemen from Baghdad. Let me see, now… Hassan, Aziz, Hammad, young Sinbad…"

"But I *am* Sinbad!" he exclaimed.

The captain looked closely at the bearded man and saw that it was indeed the young merchant he'd abandoned months before.

They embraced, with many tears.

The captain helped Sinbad sell his merchandise at such a handsome profit that, when he returned home, Sinbad was laden down with riches. With his new-found wealth, he soon forgot the hardships he'd endured.

And yet… as days passed into months, Sinbad the Sailor missed the sea. It wasn't long before he embarked on a second voyage – even more amazing than the first.

Second
Voyage

ABANDONED

With a fair wind in the sails, Sinbad set out again. The ship made good progress and, after several weeks, put in for fresh provisions on a deserted shore.

This island was blessed with fruit trees, babbling brooks and cheery birdsong. Rare blossom laid its scent upon the air like fragrant musk. Overcome by the heady perfume, Sinbad sat beneath a tree and fell into the sweetest slumber.

When he awoke – horror of horrors! – the ship had sailed off without him.

"Miserable fool!" he cried, beating his head. "Why did I have to go to sea again?"

To get a better view of his new home, he climbed a tall tree and looked around. Nothing but sky and water, tree and sand.

But wait! What was that gleaming in the distance? A dazzling white dome taller than twenty palaces! As he came closer, he saw it was too smooth to climb and had no window or door. What could it be?

THE ROOKH EGG

All at once, a black cloud blotted out the sun, turning day to night. Looking up, he saw it wasn't a cloud at all, but a giant bird. Each of its flapping wings was as broad as a mainsail, its legs were like tree-trunks, its beak as long as a man-of-war.

Then Sinbad recalled an old salt's tale of a monster bird, a rookh, that fed its young on elephants. This must be a rookh's egg.

The bird flew down, covering the egg and Sinbad too. As he lay trembling beneath its wings, a desperate plan hatched in his head.

"What if I unwind my turban and tie one end to my waist, the other to the bird's leg? When it flies off, it will take me with it."

Night passed and, as the sun rose above the trees, the bird flew up with a deafening squawk. Higher and higher it soared, until Sinbad feared it would bump its head on Heaven's roof. Then it dropped like a stone, driving his stomach into his mouth, and landed gently on a rock.

This was Sinbad's chance. Quickly, he untied his turban and slid down behind the rock. From his hiding-place he could see the rookh peering about. What was it looking for?

He didn't have long to wait. The bird swooped down upon a serpent as big as a minaret. Seizing the prey in its talons, the bird flapped off across the mountain tops.

Sinbad looked around in dismay: he was now in a treeless valley ringed by crags that pierced the sky. But… what was that sparkling in the sun? Here… over there… everywhere – the ground was strewn with diamonds!

DIAMOND VALLEY

One moment Sinbad's eyes were shining with joy. The next...
he froze in terror.

Coiled about the diamonds were hundreds of squirming snakes
big enough to swallow a caravan of camels. Seeing Sinbad, they hissed
loudly and flicked out red tongues as they slithered towards him.

What was he to do?

Slowly he edged towards the mountain wall, seeking a crevice in
which to hide. But a black, scaly brute fixed him with its stare, pinning
him to the spot. As it opened its jaws to swallow him...

C-R-A-S-H !

To Sinbad's amazement, a dead sheep landed right beside him,
and the serpent slithered away. Looking up, he saw, high above,
faces gazing down.

Of course! They must be hunters – dropping meat to stick
to the diamonds. If they were lucky, a rookh would seize the meat
and carry it to a crag, where they would scare the rookh away.
The diamonds would then be theirs.

This gave Sinbad an idea. Stuffing his pockets with the largest gems, he hid beneath the sheep and waited. It was not long before he felt himself being lifted up and whisked through the air to a lofty crag. Before the bird could rip up the meat, however, a terrible din rent the air.

Bong-bong-bong! Crash-crash!

Donggg-donggg! Pee-ee-eep-pee-ee-eep!

Bells, cymbals, gongs and whistles!

The rookh took off in fright, leaving its prey behind.

Imagine the hunters' shock when they came for their prize!
But Sinbad calmed their fears, telling them his story and sharing out
the gems. In return, the hunters led him down the mountain to
a busy port, where he joined a ship for Basra.

At last Sinbad came home with his diamonds, and he began to live
like a sheikh. But… the call of the sea was as strong as ever. And it was
not long before he made a third voyage even more remarkable than
the first two.

Third Voyage

THE ISLE OF APES

This time Fate was unkind. Not long out of Basra, Sinbad's ship ran into a fierce storm that blew it off course. Closer and closer it drifted towards a forbidding shore. "All is lost!" wailed the captain. "That is the terrible Isle of Apes!"

Even as he was tearing his hair, the vessel ran aground with a shuddering crash. In an instant it was swarming with hairy brown apes. They clambered up the rigging and tossed the men overboard, mocking them with cruel yellow eyes. Those who managed to swim ashore stared in disbelief as the apes hoisted the mainsail and sailed away.

The men were marooned. There was nothing for it but to seek food and shelter on the island.

The survivors hadn't walked far when, in the gathering gloom, they sighted a palace surrounded by a high stone wall. It looked deserted. So they ventured through the courtyard and into the main hall.

In the centre of the vast hall stood
a cooking pot and iron spits above
glowing embers. All around were piles
of bones, picked clean and stinking
as foully as camel dung.

Suddenly, the men felt the ground
shake beneath their feet, and a roar
like thunder blasted their ears.
Into the palace came the most hideous
giant ogre. Spotting the intruders,
his eyes blazed like burning coals
and he smacked his lips hungrily.

THE OGRE'S FEAST

Sinbad and his companions cowered in a corner as, one by one, the monster picked them up between finger and thumb, inspecting them as a butcher might a herd of cattle at market. Most were tossed aside – too lean for a meal.

When he came to the captain – a fat, fleshy man – the monster gave a grunt of pleasure. Skewering the man on a spit, he hung it above the fire, now and then turning it to roast evenly. When the meat was done, it disappeared – *gollop-gollop-gollop* – in three noisy mouthfuls. The ogre belched loudly, then cracked and sucked the bones.

Having eaten, he locked the door, stretched out on a bench and was soon snoring loudly.

Half-dead with terror, the men waited through the night. At the crack of dawn, the ogre rose and went out, locking the door behind him.

"What are we to do?" a sailor wailed. "Better to drown at sea than end up as monkey food," groaned another. "Wait, shipmates," cried Sinbad. "I have an idea." As the men crowded round, he explained his plan.

At sunset, a boom like a thunder clap announced the ogre's coming. No sooner had he entered than he seized a plump merchant – who was duly spitted, roasted and gobbled up. Then, as before, the ogre lay down to sleep.

This was their chance. At Sinbad's signal, the men thrust the pair of iron spits into the fire until they were red hot. Then, with twelve men holding each ramrod, they ran full tilt at the snoring ogre. With all their force they plunged the red-hot irons into his eyes.

"Aaarrrhhh! Aaarrrhhh!" The wounded beast uttered an agonised roar and lashed out blindly left and right. Then he crashed through the door and rushed down to the sea to douse the flames.

ESCAPE BY RAFT

Warily, the sailors followed at a distance. But they soon lost sight of the wounded ogre. Without his eyes, they reckoned, he surely couldn't harm them any more.

As fast as they could, the men started to make rafts for their escape, uprooting trees and binding them together with strong fibre. But just as the rafts were ready, the ground shook more violently than ever.

Oh no!

The blinded beast was stumbling along the shore. And he was not alone. Guiding him was an ogress even more hideous than himself.

The men hurriedly launched their rafts as the two ogres rushed towards them. Alas! Few made it to the open sea. For the beasts hurled rocks and boulders, crushing almost every craft. It was a miracle that Sinbad and two companions survived, as rocks fell like giant hailstones all about them. Furiously they paddled out of range and, exhausted by their efforts, abandoned themselves to the mercy of the waves.

When they awoke, they found themselves out of sight of the Isle of Apes. They were alone on the vast ocean, with no food or water or rescue in sight. Thus they drifted for several days and nights until – Allah be praised – they sighted sails on the horizon. Leaping up and down, they waved and yelled like madmen.

This time Fate was kind. The ship spotted them and changed course to pick them up. Within a few weeks Sinbad was back home in Baghdad. Though poor in pocket, he was greeted joyfully by his family and friends, who thought he had perished. Slowly but surely, rest worked its balm upon his spirit and he made plans to recover his fortune.

Little did he know that his fourth voyage was to be even more extraordinary than the three before.

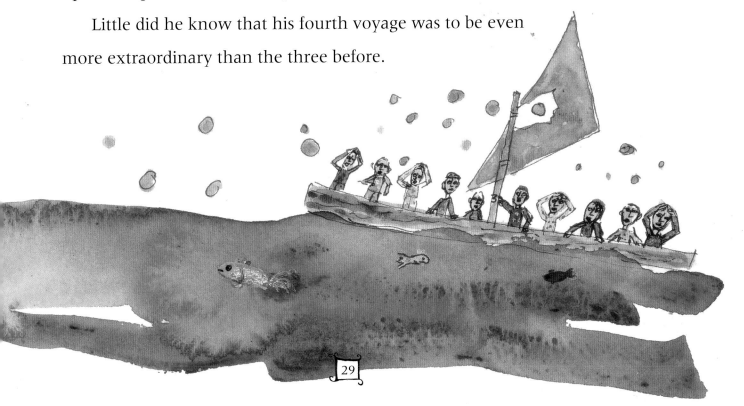

Fourth Voyage

CANNIBALS

The fourth voyage started out well enough: the sea was calm and Sinbad traded with fair profit at each port of call. Then, in mid-ocean, a ferocious wind suddenly lifted up the sea and hurled clashing waves against the ship. All hands were swept overboard. Those who survived were tossed like flotsam on the towering swell, until wind and tide cast them upon a sandy shore.

In no time at all, the half-drowned sailors were surrounded by a horde of dark-skinned men babbling away in a strange tongue. Hungry and tired, the men were led before the local king.

To their relief, the king made them welcome, ordering trayfuls of sweetmeats to be set before the guests. The men ate hungrily. As for Sinbad, his stomach was so weak, he couldn't touch the food; he looked on enviously as his shipmates set about the tasty dishes.

But how odd! The more they ate, the more they craved. The men stuffed their bellies like snuffling pigs… and as they ate, their stomachs grew and grew to the size of pumpkins. Little did Sinbad know that his lack of appetite would save his life. For he and his companions had fallen among cannibals who fattened their prisoners before eating them. Those who weren't killed and roasted were led off to pasture like wild animals. Sinbad was put out to graze with the others. But when the herdsman's back was turned, he slipped away, hiding in the trees. Fear drove him on, and he stumbled through the jungle for six days and nights without rest.

SINBAD'S WEDDING

On the morning of the seventh day, Sinbad arrived at the shore and met up with a party of sailors. Thankfully, he sailed with them, so escaping from Cannibal Island.

When his new ship put into port, Sinbad set out in search of work. Fortune went with him, for, as an honoured guest, he was led before the king and treated kindly. To repay the king's hospitality, Sinbad made him a wooden saddle padded with leather and decorated with gold and silken tassels. The king was delighted. "I must reward you!" he exclaimed.

Expecting gold or jewels, Sinbad was surprised when a beautiful princess was led in. "You shall take my youngest daughter for your wife," the king declared. Sinbad could not refuse. He was soon married and living in a grand palace with servants, slaves and all his heart could desire.

For several years he lived a life of luxury and bliss, loving his wife as deeply as she loved him.

Alas! Who can foresee what is to come? One day his neighbour's wife died. Sinbad did his best to comfort the grieving man. "Cheer up! May Allah grant you long life and an even lovelier wife."

But the man was inconsolable.

"My friend," he sighed, "you do not understand. I must be buried with my dead wife. Such is our custom."

Sinbad followed the funeral procession to a hilltop above the sea. On the summit was a stone covering a deep hole. Rolling back the stone, servants lowered the coffin, followed by the husband on a long rope. Tied to his back were seven loaves and a water jug.

Sinbad grew sick with fear. What if *his* wife died? "No, no," he told himself. "She's far too young. I am bound to die first."

Shortly after, however, his wife fell sick and died. On his knees, Sinbad begged the king to spare him. But custom pardoned no man. Ropes were tied beneath his arms and, with bread and water to last him just seven days, Sinbad was lowered with the coffin into the Cave of the Dead. The stone was replaced and he was left there to die.

THE CAVE OF THE DEAD

In the glimmer of light from above, Sinbad saw all around him
crumbling coffins and dead bodies, some new, some mouldy with decay.

"O Sinbad of the restless soul," he wailed. "Why did you
not stay at home?"

For several days he lived on bread and water, growing accustomed to the foul smell and sleeping in a space cleared of bones. In the end his food ran out and he resigned himself to death.

Just then, however, the stone shifted and a coffin dropped down, accompanied by a frail old man. The old man died within the hour, leaving his loaves and water behind. So Sinbad survived for another week.

No more coffins fell. Once more Sinbad closed his eyes and surrendered his soul to Allah. But… Oh no! Would he never be granted peace to die?

He caught a distant sound – of snuffling and scampering feet.

With a sigh, he rose and followed the noise, stumbling past skeletons, rotting shrouds and matted spider webs. At last he glimpsed a fleeting shadow and – Allah be praised – a dim light in the distance. What could it be?

Of course! Rats or foxes must have burrowed through in search
of food! Following the light, he soon found himself outside the cave,
joyfully breathing in the cool, fresh air.

He was standing at the foot of a tall cliff. For the next few days
he fed off birds' eggs, seaweed and berries, drinking from rain-filled
pools. Meanwhile, he collected up bundles of treasure from the tomb,
in case of escape.

His charmed life continued. A passing ship sighted him on the shore
and a boat was sent to pick him up. Within a few weeks he arrived
home, after sharing his treasure with the crew. How overjoyed
his family was to see him safe and laden down with treasure!
He gave generously to the poor and began to live a life of leisure.

But… a strange illness afflicts the rich, making them wish
to become yet richer. So it was with Sinbad. He was soon planning
a fifth voyage that was to be the most amazing of them all.

Fifth Voyage

REVENGE

Sinbad's fifth voyage went well for a time… until his ship put in at a small island for fresh water.

While Sinbad stayed on board, the other sailors went ashore and had great fun throwing stones at a large white dome.

Little did they know it was a rookh egg. Smashing the shell, they killed the baby rookh and returned, boasting of their sport.

Sinbad was horrified. "We are doomed," he cried. "The parents are bound to seek revenge."

Making haste for the open sea, the sailors had scarcely covered a dozen leagues before two huge storm clouds obscured the sun. As the clouds approached, the men heard the beating of wings

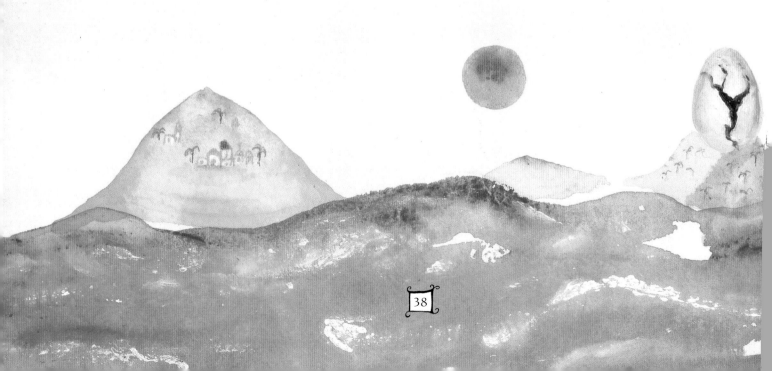

and cries more dreadful than a thousand thunder-claps. Looking up, they saw to their horror two rookhs, holding in their talons rocks larger than the ship.

As one boulder fell, the captain swung the tiller sharply – and it missed by a whisker, leaving a hole so deep they could see the sea-bed. But a second rock landed amidships – *KER – R – RASH!* Those who were not crushed to death were swept into the foaming sea and dragged under by a whirlpool.

Once again, Sinbad's charmed life saved him from a watery grave. Hauling himself astride a log, he paddled hard with hands and feet, and finally reached land, more dead than alive.

But what land! When he opened his eyes, he thought he was in Paradise.

THE OLD MAN OF THE SEA

When Sinbad felt well enough to explore his new home, he was surprised to find that he was not alone. There, on a bank below a waterfall, sat an old man. The skinny, wrinkled figure was naked save for a skirt of vine leaves and long straggly hair.

"Ahoy there, shipmate!" called Sinbad cheerily.

The old man nodded, making signs that he wanted to be carried across the stream.

Mindful of a place in heaven for those who help the poor, Sinbad took the old man upon his shoulders and waded to the far bank.

But when he went to set him down, the old man twisted his legs round Sinbad's neck and squeezed so hard, he could hardly breathe. Each time Sinbad sank to his knees, exhausted by the load, the old man struck him with a stick. With hefty blows on back and shoulders, he directed Sinbad to right and left, like a mule.

His cruel taskmaster did not dismount by night or day. Whenever he wished to sleep, he'd wind his legs tighter round Sinbad's neck and doze like a camel. Then Sinbad would snatch the chance to rest. But not for long. The old man would soon wake up and beat him without mercy.

So it went on for months on end, until one day Sinbad noticed some large gourds beneath a trailing vine. While the old man was slumbering,

he picked up an empty gourd and filled it with juice squeezed from grapes. This he left in the sun until it turned to wine. Each morning, as the old man slept, he took a sip to refresh himself.

On one occasion, however, the old man opened his eyes just as Sinbad was drinking. Straight away he made signs demanding a drink. When Sinbad offered him the gourd, he greedily drained it.

This was exactly what Sinbad had planned. In no time at all the old man's eyes began to roll, his arms flapped and his legs relaxed their grip. With a sudden tilt forward, Sinbad sent him sprawling to the ground in a drunken sleep.

Free at last, Sinbad ran to the seashore where he found sailors collecting fresh water. Hearing his tale, they cried in amazement, "That was the Old Man of the Sea. No one has ever escaped from him before!"

COCONUTS AND PEARLS

Sinbad went aboard and after many days, the ship put in at a busy port for the merchants to trade.

Before Sinbad went in search of work, a friendly merchant gave him this advice: "Take a sack and a linen bag. Fill the bag with pebbles. Go beyond the town to a valley of coconut palms. Throw the pebbles at the monkeys you see in the trees there. Then stand well back..."

Sinbad was puzzled by these words. But he had nothing to lose, so he took a sack and linen bag, filled the bag with pebbles and walked through the town.

Just as the merchant had said, the trees were
swarming with monkeys.

"Here goes!" cried Sinbad, hurling his pebbles.

Enraged by the shower of stones, the monkeys
paid him back… with coconuts! Sinbad had to be quick
on his feet, dodging this way and that to avoid
a cracked skull. Now he realised what the sack
was for. Filling it up, he took the coconuts
to market and sold the lot.

The coconut shy went on each day for several weeks – until Sinbad had enough money to buy cinnamon, peppers and aloe-wood. With this trade, he paid for his passage to a nearby bay where he hired men to dive for pearls. In the passing of time, he earned a small fortune – enough to return home to Baghdad richer than ever before.

As always, his family was overjoyed to see him, and he settled down to a life of peace and contentment. But… who can explain a sailor's heart? It wasn't long before he made a sixth voyage – an adventure so incredible you'll forget all the tales that went before.

Sixth Voyage

THE AMBER STREAM

On his sixth voyage, Sinbad was enjoying new sights, trading from port to port, and growing richer by the day.

How luck can swiftly change! One day, as the ship was passing jagged reefs, a sudden squall overtook them, striking the ship full in the face. Giant waves overturned the vessel and all hands were drowned – except for Sinbad.

His charmed life continued. He managed to swim past the reef to the foot of sheer cliffs. Wherever he looked, the shore was littered with shipwrecks and washed-up treasure. As he picked his way along the strand, he came to a stream flowing out of the lofty cliff.

When he looked closer, he could scarcely believe his eyes: the river-bed was glittering with diamonds!

And that wasn't all. Down the middle of the stream flowed amber the colour of burnished ebony. As the stream met the sea, fish drank it greedily, and later spat it out as ambergris. This sweet scent filled the air.

Sinbad smiled grimly to himself. "These treasures are worthless," he sighed, "since no one can escape." For on one side were impassable cliffs, on the other jagged reefs.

Then an idea entered his head.

"That stream must have a source… It has to flow through the rock."

He set to, gathering aloe branches and binding them together with fibre. Then, loading his raft with sacks of ambergris and diamonds, he set off, using ship's poles for oars.

The raft drifted with the flow into a dark tunnel whose low roof forced Sinbad to lie flat to avoid being crushed. Worn out by his efforts, he fell into a deep sleep.

When he opened his eyes – Allah be praised – he was lying on sun-warmed grass. But all around, dark-skinned men were staring down at him.

THE LAND OF SARANDIP

"Peace be with you, stranger," someone said. "You are in the land of Sarandip. We saw your raft and brought it to the bank."

Sinbad told the story of his adventures and the men were astounded. They led him to their king, so that he could hear the stories for himself. When he had presented the King of Sarandip with gifts of diamonds and ambergris, Sinbad began:

"I am from Baghdad, City of Peace. It is ruled by Caliph Harun al-Rashid, Prince of Believers…" And he related his adventures.

The king was so entranced by the stories and impressed by Baghdad's mighty ruler that he said to Sinbad, "I shall send your Caliph a gift worthy of the Prince of Believers."

Some days later, Sinbad was summoned to take the king's offerings to Baghdad. The gift was truly magnificent – a ruby vase filled with pearls as big as chestnuts, a magic snakeskin, two hundred camphor balls, a pair of elephant tusks… and a beautiful dancing girl.

Bidding the king farewell, Sinbad set sail in a ship waiting at the harbour. Through the mercy of Allah, he came safely to Baghdad and went straight to the Caliph. Kissing the ground between his hands and delivering the gifts, he told the Caliph about the King of Sarandip. "He is worthy of your friendship, O Caliph," he said.

Having done his duty, Sinbad hurried home to his family, with no thought of further adventure. After all, he was no longer a headstrong sailor eager to face any danger. At last he was content to plant his feet firmly on his hearth.

But Fate willed differently. The delighted Caliph commanded Sinbad to take gifts back to the King of Sarandip. And this final voyage was to be more amazing than all the rest put together.

Seventh Voyage

SEA MONSTER

Reluctantly, Sinbad undertook his seventh voyage, bearing the Caliph's gifts to the King of Sarandip. He duly fulfilled his mission and was returning home when, all at once, the ship rose in the air as if lifted by a giant's hand. Next moment, it crashed back to the sea. A roar more terrible than thunder deafened the crew. Coming towards them, its mouth open like a valley between two hills, was a sea-monster as big as a mountain! It leapt from a towering wave and in a single mouthful swallowed half the ship – from stern to foremast.

Sinbad just had time to dive into the sea

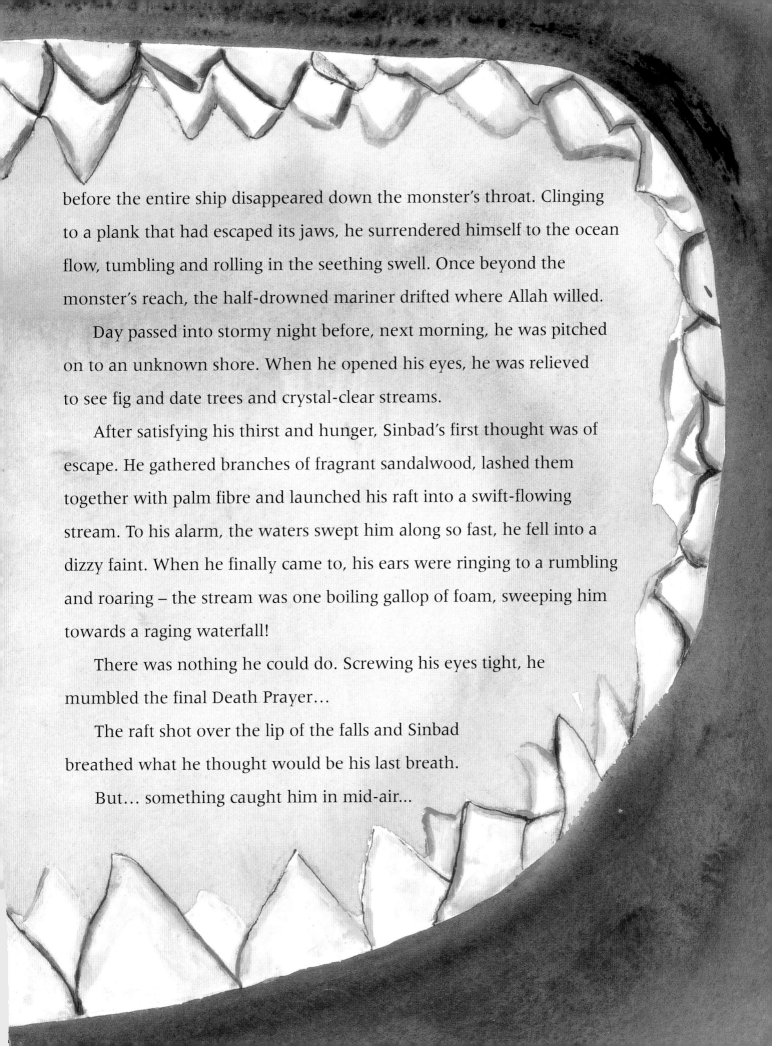

before the entire ship disappeared down the monster's throat. Clinging to a plank that had escaped its jaws, he surrendered himself to the ocean flow, tumbling and rolling in the seething swell. Once beyond the monster's reach, the half-drowned mariner drifted where Allah willed.

Day passed into stormy night before, next morning, he was pitched on to an unknown shore. When he opened his eyes, he was relieved to see fig and date trees and crystal-clear streams.

After satisfying his thirst and hunger, Sinbad's first thought was of escape. He gathered branches of fragrant sandalwood, lashed them together with palm fibre and launched his raft into a swift-flowing stream. To his alarm, the waters swept him along so fast, he fell into a dizzy faint. When he finally came to, his ears were ringing to a rumbling and roaring – the stream was one boiling gallop of foam, sweeping him towards a raging waterfall!

There was nothing he could do. Screwing his eyes tight, he mumbled the final Death Prayer…

The raft shot over the lip of the falls and Sinbad breathed what he thought would be his last breath.

But… something caught him in mid-air...

AUCTION

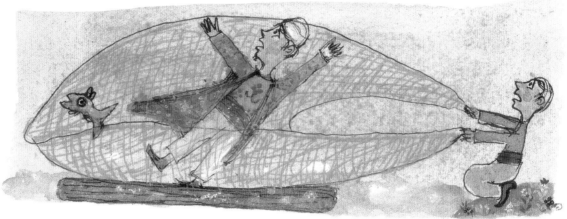

Sinbad was ensnared in a fisherman's net!

When he was cut free, he was taken to a merchant's house to recover. After three days of rest his host said, "Now you are well again, I advise you to sell your merchandise. It is a rarity in these parts."

Sinbad was puzzled. What merchandise? He'd been cast naked among these people. Dumbly, he followed his host to market and was surprised to see his raft surrounded by merchants nodding wisely and waggling their beards. From all sides came such exclamations as, "By Allah, what wonderful wood!" "Never have I seen such sandalwood!"

Soon the auctioneer opened the bidding – at a thousand dinars.

"Two thousand."

"Three."

The bidding closed at ten.

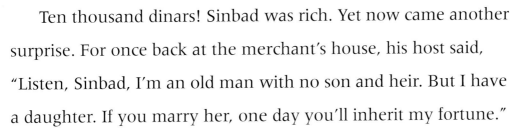

Ten thousand dinars! Sinbad was rich. Yet now came another surprise. For once back at the merchant's house, his host said, "Listen, Sinbad, I'm an old man with no son and heir. But I have a daughter. If you marry her, one day you'll inherit my fortune."

Remembering the fate of his last wife, Sinbad politely refused. But the old man begged him, so finally Sinbad said with a sigh, "I owe you so much, my friend, that if it will make you happy, then I agree."

The kahdi and witnesses were called without delay and the wedding was held.

Within a year, the old man passed away into Allah's mercy. Sinbad now had a beautiful wife and more wealth than he'd ever known. What more could a man wish for?

THE LAST ADVENTURE

Sinbad was happy in his new life. Yet one thing worried him. Each spring, the men of the city sprouted wings and flew up to the sky. No one would tell him why.

At last, by bribing a neighbour, Sinbad was able to experience the thrill of flying – clinging to his neighbour's back. So high did they fly, that Sinbad heard the angels singing under Heaven's vaulted dome.

He couldn't help himself. "Praise be to Allah!" he cried out.

Hardly had the words left his mouth, than the winged man threw off his passenger, and Sinbad fell through the air like a stone. He would have been ground to dust had he not landed on a snowy mountain-top.

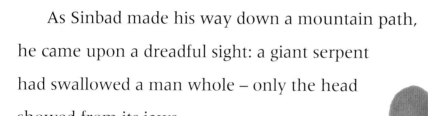

As Sinbad made his way down a mountain path, he came upon a dreadful sight: a giant serpent had swallowed a man whole – only the head showed from its jaws.

'Save me! Save me!' the head cried. At once Sinbad killed the serpent with a rock and pulled the man free.

To his surprise, he saw it was his neighbour.

"I threw you off because you mentioned the Name," the man explained. "Never speak it again."

With that, he took Sinbad upon his back and in the twinkling of an eye they were back in Sinbad's courtyard. When Sinbad described the strange adventure to his wife, she declared, "My father always warned me of these people. They are worshippers of Shaitan, the Devil. We must leave at once."

Sinbad lost no time in selling his property, buying rich merchandise and hiring a ship to take him and his wife to Baghdad. He was going home with some misgivings. After all, many years had passed since he'd last left. Was his first wife still alive? Would his children still recognise him?

He need not have worried. His first wife was overjoyed to see him and welcomed his second wife as generously as she did him.

Twenty-seven long years had passed since Sinbad's first voyage. He was now content to sit at home and tell his amazing adventures to his many grandchildren. He vowed never, ever to go to sea again.

And – Allah be praised! – he never did.

ABOUT THE STORY

Sinbad's seven voyages are filled with the most fantastic adventures. No seafarer has ever undertaken such amazing journeys – except perhaps Jason in his search for the Golden Fleece.

Who was Sinbad? We know that he was a merchant living in Baghdad during the reign of Caliph Harun al-Rashid (789-809), that his seven voyages took 27 years, and that his story was one of many told by the wise Shahrazad, wife of Sultan Shah Ryar.

Once upon a time, so the story goes, the Sultan had a dream in which his first wife was unfaithful. So jealous was he, that he vowed, "Each time I take a wife, she shall die before the night is out. I shall never be deceived again!"

Thus it was. Each new wife was beheaded at sunrise. Finally he married Shahrazad, who devised a clever plan: each night she would tell the Sultan a story. At dawn, she would break off at the most exciting part. So eager was the Sultan to hear the story's end that he kept sparing her, night after night.

This went on for 1001 nights. At last, the Sultan renounced his vow and ordered his scribes to write down Shahrazad's wonderful tales in letters of gold so that everyone might enjoy them. They filled thirty volumes and became known as *The Book of the Thousand and One Nights*. Some know them as *The Arabian Nights*. They include such familiar stories as Aladdin and his Wonderful Lamp, Ali Baba and the Forty Thieves, The Adventures of Harun al-Rashid, The Fisherman and the Bottle – and, of course, Sinbad the Sailor.

Sinbad and the other tales were passed on down the ages, retold by storytellers in palaces and market squares throughout the Middle East, China and India. According to the great 19th-century traveller and scholar Sir Richard Burton, some stories date back

to the 8th century, though the whole work took final shape five
centuries later. There was no single author, for the *Nights* were
the work of several writers, all unknown.

The stories reached Europe in the early 18th century in a French
translation of an Egyptian text dating back to the 14th century.
The first English version appeared in 1792. Since then, Aladdin,
Ali Baba – and above all, Sinbad – have entertained us all in books,
films, pantomime and music.

GLOSSARY

Allah	Muslim name for God
aloe-wood	highly-prized wood from an oriental tree used in medicine
ambergris	sweet-smelling wax from a whale's stomach, sometimes found floating in tropical seas
caliph	Muslim ruler
camphor	strong-smelling white crystal used in medicine and to repel moths
Death Prayer	Muslim prayer chanted over a person who has just died
dinar	currency used in many parts of the Middle East
kahdi	Muslim chief judge
the Name	Allah
Prince of Believers	chief of all Muslim believers. Here it means Harun al-Rashid, Caliph of Baghdad from 789 to 809
rookh	a monstrous mythical bird
Shaitan	Muslim name for the Devil

The Isle of Apes

Sea Monster

Whale Island

Diamond Valley

Rookh Island